The Girl who Dared

By Shirin Shamsi
Illustrated by Felia Hanakata

Publishing Credits

Rachelle Cracchiolo, M.S.Ed., *Publisher*
Conni Medina, M.A.Ed., *Editor in Chief*
Nika Fabienke, Ed.D., *Content Director*
Véronique Bos, *Creative Director*
Shaun N. Bernadou, *Art Director*
Carol Huey-Gatewood, M.A.Ed., *Editor*
Valerie Morales, *Associate Editor*
Kevin Pham, *Graphic Designer*

Image Credits

Illustrated by Felia Hanakata

5301 Oceanus Drive
Huntington Beach, CA 92649-1030
www.tcmpub.com

ISBN 978-1-6449-1328-4

Table of Contents

Chapter One: The Bike · · · · · · · · · · 5

Chapter Two: The Parting · · · · · · · 11

Chapter Three: On the Run · · · · · 17

Chapter Four: Escape! · · · · · · · · 23

Chapter Five: Safe at Last? · · · · · · · 27

About Us · · · · · · · · · · · · · · · · · · 32

CHAPTER ONE

The Bike

Rukia stepped outside. She moved quietly toward the shed. No one would choose to leave the cool house for the humid outdoors. No one but Rukia, who yearned for adventure. The wooden door creaked as she pulled it open. She sighed with relief to see no one was there as she opened the

wooden door wide. Looking over
her shoulder once again, Rukia made
sure there was no one watching. Ami
was resting with the baby. Papa
was away with Rukia's older brother,
Atif. Babu had gone to fetch her five-
year-old brother, Noni, who was at a
friend's house.

Rukia grabbed the servant's bike
from the shed and wheeled it out. She
paused to carefully close the door, and
then she was off. Rukia rode the bike
down the lane of the family *haveli*. The
enclosure spread out as far and as wide
as her eyes could see. Her family had
lived here for as long as the banyan
trees grew, perhaps even longer.

As the afternoon sun burned down
on her, Rukia smiled, turning her face
up to greet its blazing warmth. She
did not care if her face turned dark
as roasted almonds, for she felt free
as a bird. Everyone in the house was
sleeping, as it was far too hot to venture
outside. She and Atif would ride

bicycles together in a few years, racing through the streets, even at night. But for now, this was the only time Rukia could get away with riding a bike. She gripped the handlebars tightly. She leaned forward and whizzed down the slope of the dirt path.

It was a bumpy ride, but Rukia did not mind. Her face glowed as her smile spread from ear to ear. Her shawl flapped behind her in the wind like the sails of a ship as the bike breezed down the lane. Rukia's cares evaporated in the wind, and she closed her eyes and imagined all the things she would do if she were free like a boy. She could do anything. No one could stop her.

Rukia's shawl caught in the wheel. Before she could stop herself, the bike toppled over. She landed clumsily in a heap in the dirt. As she rubbed her bruised knee, tears of frustration filled her eyes. She was glad no one saw her covered in dirt. This dirt, this earth, was part of India. In a few days, with the signing of documents by some men in an office, it would become a new land—the Republic of Pakistan. She would live in a new country without even leaving her home.

Rukia looked at her home, the

haveli, as it loomed tall in the distance. Trees surrounded it, and flowers bloomed in terra-cotta pots along the wide veranda. The heavy scent of jasmine filled the air. Rukia took a deep breath. She felt safe here, though there was unrest in the country. Rukia shook the dirt off her clothing. She picked up the bike and made her way back before everyone awoke.

CHAPTER TWO

The Parting

Rukia tiptoed inside the house. Something was amiss, for Papa was there with her mother, Ami, and he never came home early. Rukia's heart lurched at the fear and worry apparent on her parents' faces. Papa's voice shook with desperation.

"We have to leave immediately,

for the sake of our children's future," he said, his voice breaking as his composure dissolved. Ami sobbed quietly.

Through her tears, she whispered, "When do we leave? How do I even pack?" She could not fathom leaving her home at a moment's notice.

"We must leave now," Papa repeated urgently. "There is no time to pack. We must leave for Chacha's home immediately. From there, we will catch the train to Lahore. The car is waiting. We need the car for you and the baby, but the driver will not wait long."

"But Noni is not home, and Babu is out on errands." Ami's voice shook. "He will bring him back on his return— surely we cannot leave now, before Noni is here."

Rukia was shocked to see Ami distraught and her strong Papa so shaken. She had never seen him so fearful. Rukia edged forward, trembling. She would try to be brave.

"Papa, why do we have to leave?" Rukia asked softly.

"The rumors were wrong," Papa sighed. "Our province of Punjab is being divided into two. Our home will no longer be part of the new country. We must leave quickly. Rioting has begun, and it is not safe. First, we go to Chacha's home, and from there we will take the train to Lahore, to the new Pakistan."

Rukia had to be brave when everything around her was uncertain. She would help her parents, no matter what needed to be done.

The plan was simple. Babu would bring Noni home from his friend's house. Rukia would tell Babu to ride them over to Chacha's house. Papa would make arrangements for the train. They could not miss the train, for tensions were running high among people on the streets, and Papa could not be convinced to stay any longer. He had said goodbye to his home, where the bones of his ancestors lay buried.

"She can't wait here," Ami said to Papa. "Atif must help us get everything to the train," said Papa, "and Babu will return soon."

"Don't worry, I will help Babu bring Noni to Chacha's house," Rukia said.

"Hurry, hurry," Papa yelled. Ami bundled baby Munir in her arms and held tightly to Atif's hand. She hugged Rukia. A sob escaped her as she turned away. They trusted Babu. He would bring Noni back from the neighboring town. Rukia watched from the window, clutching her hands together.

"Be brave, my *Bety*," Papa said as he hugged Rukia tightly. Rukia did not want him to leave. She did not want her world to change.

CHAPTER THREE

On the Run

Rukia watched with a sinking heart as her parents and brothers drove away. She was alone. As soon as her parents left, the servants began to gather their belongings. They would not stay. There was talk of riots, they told her.

Fear hung heavy in the air as Rukia waited for Babu and her little brother.

She hoped Babu would bring Noni home soon so they could leave in time to catch the train—the train that would take them to their new homeland.

She stood by the window as the sun sank below the horizon. The sound of the muezzin's call to prayer echoed in the distance above the treetops from the mosque's pointed minaret. Babu and Noni were late. It was getting dark. Then, Rukia saw Babu stagger across the path with Noni. Where was his motorbike?

Rukia ran out the front door and down the path. Little Noni was shaking like a leaf. His grubby face was tear-stained, and his lower lip quivered at the sight of her. Horrified, she watched as Babu limped toward her, holding tightly onto Noni. She gasped when she saw that Babu's torn shirt was stained with blood.

"What happened?" Rukia whispered, her voice shaky.

"They took the bike," Noni said

through his tears. "They beat Babu."
His face was covered in grime.

"Who did this?" Rukia asked, her
voice breaking as she clutched Noni's
hand and helped Babu.

"The streets are unsafe—hordes of
rioters gather to make trouble," Babu
said weakly.

"Don't worry, *Beta*," said Babu
patting Noni's head. "We are safe now."

Together, they hobbled into the

house. Rukia held on to Noni while Babu held her arm.

"But how will we get to Chacha's?" Rukia asked nervously.

"I'm sorry, but we cannot go anywhere tonight," said Babu, holding his head in pain as he shakily sat down. "There's too much rioting going on outside."

"But we have to," said Rukia, stunned. Babu had been with her family since Papa was a boy. He had grown up in the *haveli*. He had lived his entire life there; he simply could not leave them at such a desperate moment. "Ami and Papa are waiting for us. Papa told me you would bring Noni back and take us to Chacha's house."

"It's too dangerous out there. I am not going anywhere," Babu said, wiping his brow. "I'm sorry, but I'm too old to leave."

"But Ami and Papa are counting on you taking us!" Rukia realized she was shouting and felt ashamed when she saw Babu turn his face away, scared and hurt. Rukia took a deep breath. She had to be strong and find courage within her. It was up to her now.

Rukia had to get her little brother to safety. She squatted down and grabbed Noni by his shoulder, looking directly at him.

"We are going on an important mission, Noni," Rukia said, her stomach queasy with fear. It took all the courage she had to sound convincing, and Noni trusted her. "Come, we must leave now, and you have to be very quiet."

She took Noni by the hand and ran with him to the bike shed.

The bike was where she had left it. Rukia picked up Noni and sat him on the second seat. She could do this. All she needed was to get to Chacha's house. It was not that far. But she had not counted on the rioting in the streets.

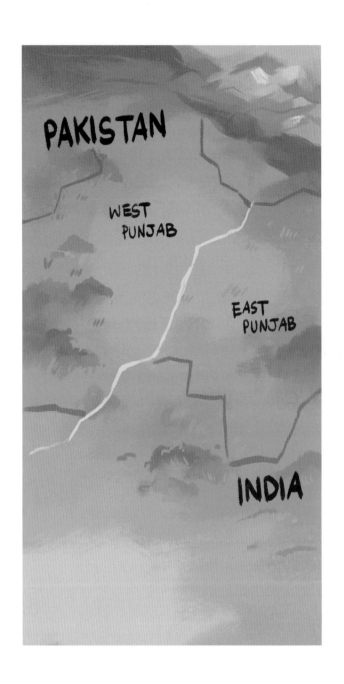

CHAPTER FOUR

Escape!

"Where's Ami?" Noni asked. He wiggled on the bicycle as Rukia kept a tight grip on the handlebars and rode toward her uncle's house.

"She's waiting for us at Chacha's house," Rukia said. "Remember what I told you? We have to be really quiet," she said, giving Noni a piece of his favorite candy from her pocket. He began chewing on the slab of *gurr*, and she hoped it would keep him content for the next few minutes.

Noni was quiet as he chewed on his candy. Noises in the streets were growing. Crowds began to gather, spilling into the road. People chanted loud slogans.

"I want Ami," Noni began to cry. "Why are people shouting?"

"Hush, Noni, I'm taking you to Ami," Rukia whispered. "We have to be very quiet so no one sees us."

She wanted no attention. Rukia hoped she could pedal, unseen, like she'd done on so many secret afternoons.

As rioting continued on the main street, Rukia turned the bike into an alley. She shivered, for it was dark and narrow. With fewer people to slow her down, she pedaled faster, taking a shortcut through to quieter streets.

She was glad she had practiced

riding the bike before, and she was glad
she knew the way to Chacha's house.
She rode bravely, with hope in her heart
that they would reach Chacha's house
in time to catch the train. She did not
stop. She was determined to get there.
She knew their lives depended on it.

CHAPTER FIVE

Safe at Last?

"Look, we're almost there, Noni," Rukia said as she breathed a sigh of relief. "Chacha's house is just around the corner."

The bike swerved as she turned onto Batala Road, where Chacha lived. It was already dark, though the full moon cast a luminous glow, as if to light her way. She kept telling herself, *Keep going!*

As they neared Chacha's house, Rukia saw plumes of smoke curling in the sky. A fire! Fear gripped Rukia, as she realized the fire was coming from Chacha's house. Rukia found the black wrought-iron gate standing wide open and the courtyard crowded with strangers hurrying with pails of water, trying desperately to put out the fire. Windows were smashed. Smoke filled the veranda.

Rukia slipped off her bike and held Noni's hand. "We're here. Ami, Papa, Chacha...?" she called.

"*Challey gay-sub challey gay*— they've gone. They've all gone," a man told her.

"I want Ami," Noni sobbed uncontrollably. He was inconsolable, though Rukia repeatedly reassured him.

"We will find Ami," Rukia said, but her heart sank, for amidst the chaos there was no sign of anyone familiar.

A girl approached them from the crowd. "It's too dangerous," she said. "They had to leave in a hurry to catch the train."

Rukia took a deep breath. She was not finished.

"The station is not far," Rukia said to Noni. Her voice quivered as she lifted

Noni back onto the bike. "We will reach Ami and Papa in no time. I will ride like the wind, you wait and see."

Rukia wheeled the bike toward the gate, turning to glance at the house one last time.

"Rukia! Noni!" a voice rang out. Papa's voice! Rukia turned and, through the smoke, she saw Papa.

He was covered in black smoke, but she could see his smile of relief as he came toward them and wrapped her and Noni in his arms.

"My brave daughter—you are my hero," Papa said through his tears.

About Us

The Author

Shirin Shamsi's parents left India for the newly created Pakistan in 1947. She was inspired by their experiences to create a story of fiction about a theme that continues to be relevant today. Refugees still journey to new lands and struggle to rebuild their lives. Shamsi was born and raised in the United Kingdom and now makes her home in the United States. When she is not writing, she enjoys reading and spending time with family.

The Illustrator

Felia Hanakata was born and raised in Bali, Indonesia. Along the way, she fell in love with drawing and filled her notebooks with sketches. One day, she dreams of writing, illustrating, and sharing her own stories with the world! When not drawing, she is usually reading, playing video games, or looking for inspiration in nature.